D0431937

2:00 3:00 4:00 5:00

Eric A. Kimmel

GRIZZ!

illustrated by
Andrew Glass

Holiday House / New York

To Iggy

E. A. K.

To Regina

A. G.

Text copyright © 2000 by Eric A. Kimmel
Illustrations copyright © 2000 by Andrew Glass
All Rights Reserved
First Edition
Printed in the United States of America

The artist used oil sticks and watercolor pencils scraped
onto the paper with plastic knives to create the illustrations.

Designed by Lynn Braswell

The text typeface is Stone Informal.

A version of this story was previously published
in *Cricket: The Magazine for Children*.

Library of Congress Cataloging-in-Publication Data
Kimmel, Eric A.
   Grizz!/by Eric A. Kimmel; illustrated by Andrew Glass.
   p. cm.
   Summary: Cowboy Lucky Doolin makes a deal with the Devil,
agreeing not to wash, shave, or change his clothes for seven years,
thus earning a fortune and the hand of his true love.
   ISBN 0-8234-1469-8
   [1. Devil—Fiction.   2. Wagers—Fiction.
3. Cowboys—Fiction.]
I. Glass, Andrew, 1949– ill.
II. Title.
PZ7.K5648Gr   2000
[E]—dc21   98-43332
CIP AC

Back in the days when an automobile was just a buggy with a gas engine and the Wright brothers were still trying to get their flying machine off the ground, there was a cowboy living over in Harney County, Oregon, by the name of Lucky Doolin.

Lucky worked on the Rocking M ranch. His boss was O.K. Madison. O.K. had a daughter, Shelby, sweet as huckleberry pie. Lucky and Shelby didn't take long to fall in love. Git married was another story.

"Clear out!" O.K. told Lucky. "Shelby weren't raised to be no cowboy's wife."

When Lucky said good-bye, Shelby gave him a ring in the shape of two hearts. Lucky swore he would wear it forever.

Lucky drifted up to Baker City, where he traded his horse for a train ticket to Denver. On the train he fell in with a smooth-talking stranger. The stranger only had half his left foot. The part that remained looked a lot like a horse's hoof.

The stranger suggested a game of poker. Lucky was willing. They played seven hands. Lucky won them all. The stranger put the cards away. "I know a better game," he said.

"How'd you like to wager your immortal soul?"

Lucky shrugged. "Why should I?"

The stranger smiled. "There's a certain young lady you want to marry. Her name's Shelby, right? You'll need cash. Lots of it. I can promise you seven years of good luck. Everything you touch will turn to money. If you win, that luck will go on until your dying day."

   "What's the catch?" Lucky knew that card-playing strangers don't make promises less'n they got their eyes on something.

   "Here it is. For seven years, starting from the minute we arrive in Denver, you don't change your clothes. You don't wash, shave your face, trim your nails, cut or comb your hair. If you can do that for seven years, your luck will last forever. But if you do any of the things aforementioned before seven years are up, then your soul belongs to me. What do you say?"

"You got a bet," said Lucky Doolin.

The train pulled into Denver at three o'clock. That evening Lucky walked into the Golden Nugget saloon. A rancher named Ike Barnes offered him a job. "It don't pay much, but room and board is free."

"Sounds okay to me," said Lucky.

Six months later Ike died. He left Lucky the ranch and $30,000 buried under the cookhouse floor.

Lucky was rich. But he wasn't done. Not nearly. That summer he dug a well. Instead of water, he struck oil. A gusher! A month later he stumbled on a creek full of yellow rocks. Gold! Lucky filed a claim on the whole mother lode.

Within a year, Lucky Doolin was the richest man in the West. Everything he touched turned to money. That stranger with the bum foot sure kept his side of the bargain. And Lucky kept his.

He still had on the rags of the clothes he wore to Denver. His hair looked like a buzzard's nest. He had a beard like a mountain man. The only time water touched his skin was when it rained.

Of course, back in those days, lots of folks tended toward the wild and wooly, so Lucky didn't attract too much attention. But by the time the fifth year rolled around, he had become distinctly unpleasant.

His smell could make a buzzard weep. He could empty out a town by walking into it. Dogs barked. Children screamed. Horses pulled up their hitching posts and galloped away.

After six years he had become a nightmare. Matted hair hung to his knees. His nails grew as long as grizzly claws. He looked like a grizzly bear. He smelled like one. So that's what folks called him: "Grizz."

The day finally came when Lucky couldn't stand no more. He didn't have no friends. The neighbors moved off. Even his dog ran away.

Only the memory of Shelby, his true love, kept him going. Lucky still wore her ring. He decided to go back to Harney County to see her one last time. Then he'd drown himself in Harney Creek and find peace at last.

Meanwhile, hard times had come to Rocking M. The ranchhouse had burned down, the cattle died, rustlers ran off the horses. Shelby and her father were as broke as a busted-down wagon. "There's good news and bad news," Parmelee Jones, the lawyer, told them. "The bad news is the mortgage on your ranch is due at three o'clock this afternoon. If you can't pay, you lose everything."

O.K. groaned. "What's the good news?"

"The good news is your aunt Agatha died. She left Shelby enough money to pay the mortgage and then some. However, there's a catch. Shelby must be married before her twenty-fifth birthday. Otherwise, she gets nothing."

"My birthday's today. I was born at three o'clock," Shelby said.

Parmelee Jones checked his watch. "You got two hours."
"There isn't anyone I want to marry," Shelby replied.
"Have you considered everyone?" Parmelee asked,
rubbing his hands together.

O.K. Madison jumped from his chair. "I know what you're thinking, you miserable weasel! You'll marry my daughter over my dead body!"

"You ain't got no choice. It's me or nothin'." Parmalee turned to Shelby. "Make up your mind, darlin'. Time's a wastin'."

Shelby faced the lawyer. "Mr. Jones, you are lower than a rattlesnake's belt buckle. However, to save our ranch, I will become your wife."

"Smart girl. I've already drawn up the papers. Sign here."

Shelby reached for the pen.

"HOLD IT RIGHT THERE!"

A thing stood in the doorway. It resembled a haystack on legs and smelled like something that should have been buried.

"They call me Grizz," the thing said. "Miss Shelby, you can't marry a skunk like Parmelee Jones. I know I look a fright, but I'll promise this. I'll disappear after the wedding. You won't ever see me again."

"No, Shelby! He's a monster!" her father cried.

Shelby didn't hesitate. "I'll marry you, Mr. Grizz."

Tears ran down the thing's hairy face. "I'll meet you at the church," it gasped. Then it ran to town to the barbershop. The barber walked with a limp. He only had half his foot.

The thing flung itself in the barber chair.

"Lucky Doolin, I've been expecting you," the barber said.

"You win, Mister. All I ask is that you clean me up and let me live long enough to put the ring on Miss Shelby's finger. Then you can do with me what you like."

"Are you sure?" the barber asked. "It's two o'clock. Seven years will be up in another hour."

"I'm sure," Lucky said. The clock struck two.

The barber snipped off a hank of hair. "That's it. I win. Your soul belongs to me."

"Hold your horses!" Lucky hollered. "I just remembered something. Colorado's an hour ahead. If it's two o'clock in Harney County, it's three o'clock in Denver. That's where we made our deal. Seven years were up when the clock struck two. That means I win!"

The barber threw down his scissors. "Bless it! I forgot about the time change!"

"Good thing I didn't!" said Lucky. "Now get busy.
Cut off this hair. Clip my nails and burn what's left of
these clothes. Then draw me a bath, hot as you can
make it. I need to soak for a spell."

Lucky Doolin made it to the church on time. He looked so good nobody recognized him. Except Shelby.

"All that hair didn't fool me. I knew it was you, even before I saw the ring," she whispered to Lucky as they walked down the aisle.

Parmelee Jones met them outside the church. "I got bad news," he snickered. "I reread Aunt Agatha's will. Shelby inherits the money unless she marries a cowboy. Then she don't get nothin'."

"Aw, who gives a hoot about Aunt Agatha!" Lucky said, throwing down a wad of thousand dollar bills. "I got enough money to pay that mortgage a hundred times over."

Lucky and Shelby bought an automobile. They drove to Yellowstone National Park for their honeymoon.

O.K. Madison told everyone he always wanted
Shelby to marry Lucky.

As for Parmelee Jones, he was last seen talking to a
stranger over by the railway station. The stranger was
missing half his left foot. That was seven years ago.
Nobody's heard from him since.

But as for Lucky Doolin and Shelby, they just went right on being in love, raising kids, getting richer every day, and living happily ever after.

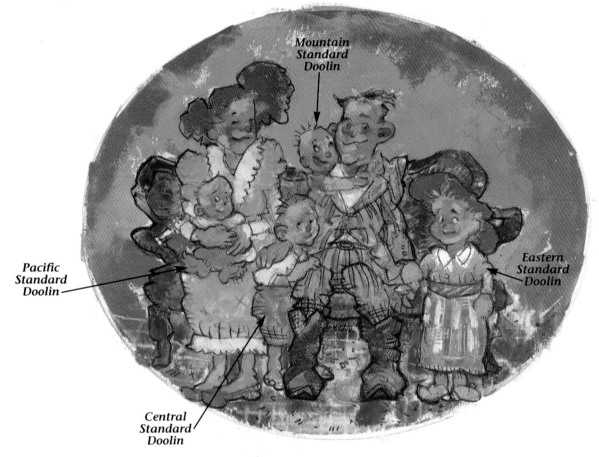

Mountain Standard Doolin

Pacific Standard Doolin

Eastern Standard Doolin

Central Standard Doolin

AUTHOR'S NOTE

The story of *Grizz!* is a cowboy version of the familiar folktale where the hero makes a bargain with the devil and gets more than he expected. My principal sources were "The Bearskin" in *Grimm's Fairy Tales* and "The Soldier Who Did Not Wash" in Charles Downing's *Russian Tales and Legends.* Also adding spice to the mix were various versions of the legend of Dr. Faustus and Stephen Vincent Benét's wonderful story, "The Devil and Daniel Webster."

In 1675 the Royal Observatory in Greenwich, England, was founded to develop a means for sailors to determine the exact position of their ships. Out of this grew a way to tell precise time at sea. But on land, local time was haphazardly based on the time of a church or town hall clock. It varied significantly between towns that were only a few miles apart. There were three hundred different local times in the United States alone!

The coming of the railroads in the 1840s underscored the need for an accurate, standardized system of telling time. The United States officially adopted the Greenwich Mean Time (GMT) at noon on November 18, 1883. The official time was sent by telegraph to all major cities. A year later the International Meridian Conference met in Washington, D.C. and established twenty-four time zones worldwide, as well as the international date line.